I WAS THERE

Viking Invasion

Published in the UK by Scholastic Children's Books, 2020
Euston House, 24 Eversholt Street, London, NW1 1DB
A division of Scholastic Limited

London ~ New York ~ Toronto ~ Sydney ~ Auckland
Mexico City ~ New Delhi ~ Hong Kong

SCHOLASTIC and associated logos are trademarks and/or
registered trademarks of Scholastic Inc.

First published in the UK by Scholastic Ltd, 2015
This edition published 2020

Text copyright © Stuart Hill, 2015

Illustrations by Michael Garton © Scholastic Ltd, 2015
Cover illustration by Ben Whitehouse © Scholastic Ltd, 2020

The right of Stuart Hill to be identified as the author of this work has been
asserted by him in accordance with the Copyright, Designs and Patents Act, 1988.

ISBN 978 1407 19789 0

A CIP catalogue record for this book is available from the British Library.

Printed and bound by CPI Group (UK) Ltd, Croydon, CR0 4YY
Papers used by Scholastic Children's Books are made from wood grown in sustainable forests.

2 4 6 8 10 9 7 5 3 1

While this book is based on real characters and actual historical events, some situations and
people are fictional, created by the author.

www.scholastic.co.uk

illustrated by
Michael Garton

I WAS THERE

Viking
Invasion

Stuart Hill

SCHOLASTIC

PROLOGUE

They're coming! The Great Viking Army is coming! They've smashed their way through France, burning cities and churches and killing thousands of people. It's said that they're the biggest army to march through Europe since the time of the Romans and no one can stand against them. Unlike many who fight them, the Great Viking Army is made up of men whose only job is to fight; conquering and killing is their job and their life. Everywhere they go they leave death and destruction behind them, and now they're coming here to the lands of the Saxons, to the land of my people and my home!

CHAPTER ONE

My name is Aldwyn, I'm eleven years old and I live in the city of Eoforwic, the capital of Northumbria – one of the most important Saxon kingdoms in all of the island of Britain. I work with my father who's a leather merchant. Like everyone who sells things to make a living, he's always watching out for anything that might stop people buying his wares. And there's nothing worse for that than armies and fighters marching through the land, especially when the fighters are the Great Viking Army.

I clearly remember the day my dad came back from dealing with the traders in the city.

He looked worried and there was something about the way he was frowning that told me it wasn't the price of leather that was bothering him. Merchants are often the first to get any news because they trade with many different areas and countries, and Dad had just heard rumours he didn't like.

I was in our main yard, packing hides into barrels ready to be sent to customers and, after he'd found that my mother wasn't at home, he came to speak to me instead.

I knew something important had happened because he didn't even pause, he just started to talk straight away. "Aldwyn, I've just heard that the Vikings are leaving France where they've been fighting for years!"

He didn't usually discuss important matters with me, so I was surprised enough to stop working. "Is that bad?" I asked.

"Well it'll be bad for whichever land they decide to attack next!"

"Yes, of course," I said, feeling guilty that I hadn't thought of the poor people who would suffer at the hands of the Vikings. "Do we know which land it'll be?"

"That's just it," Dad said, looking even more worried. "The rumours are that it'll be here."

I felt a cold chill pass through me and the hair stood up on the back of my neck. "When?" I asked quietly.

Dad shrugged. "No one knows. This year, next… Some merchants just back from France have reported that the French King has re-armed all the towns and he has fleets of ships on the rivers. Some say the Vikings are having to fight their way out, others that the French are driving them out. But whatever happens, the word is the next port of call for their ships will be here."

"Here?" I whispered, my mouth going dry. "Do you mean this city, Eoforwick?"

"I can't say, it could be anywhere on this island, but there's as much chance of it being here as anywhere else."

I nodded and, having nothing more to say and nothing better to do, I carried on packing the hides into barrels.

Dad stood in silence for a moment then said: "Anyway, where's your mother? I need to discuss things with her."

"She's gone to the market," I answered quietly. "She said something about needing some new thread."

He headed for the gate immediately, leaving me to think about what I'd been told.

Not long after this we got a message that was the beginning of the events that would change our lives for ever. We'd just had a delivery of cow skins and, even though it was the beginning of winter and freezing cold, their stink filled the entire place. The smell of them even reached the tanning sheds, where the raw skins would have their hair scraped off and then be soaked in huge barrels full of water and oak bark that would slowly turn them into leather.

The message came from my Aunt Matilda who was married to a cordwainer, or shoe maker, in Norwic in the Kingdom of the Saxons called East Anglia. It was short and simple. 'The Viking Army has landed and could march north.'

Dad said that my aunt and everyone else was fairly safe in East Anglia because their king had paid the Vikings something called

'Danegeld', which just meant he'd given them gold and money to stop them killing people and fighting.

He and my mother, Theowin, then discussed what to do and eventually, after hours of talking, they decided that my mother would go to the kingdom of Wessex. There she'd help to set up a new tannery in partnership with my father's brother, Uncle Cerdic. My sisters, Cwen and Meryl, would also go with her where they'd be safe. Wessex is a powerful kingdom with many markets and customers for fine leather, and it lies far to the south – the opposite direction to where the Viking Army was likely to go.

It was also decided that I'd stay in Eoforwic with my father and help him to run the business we still had in the city. There was little point in losing trade if you didn't have to. After all, the Vikings might go elsewhere and leave us in peace.

CHAPTER TWO

Before my mother and sisters left for Wessex, our lives continued as normal for a while. I spent my days helping Father and the workers in the tannery where the raw skins were turned into leather and then sold to the craftsmen who use it to make shoes, clothes and even things like buckets. We also make something called vellum, which is a very fine sort of leather that's used in the making of books. This we mainly sell to the cathedral, where there's a library and a scriptorium – a place where books are made, written and illuminated with beautiful pictures.

Anyway, it's all hard work and I was always glad when Sunday came and we had the day of rest – the Sabbath – that the church demanded we all had.

Some of the day was spent in the huge cathedral where we attended a service called Mass. The cathedral was beautiful and was one of the few places made of stone in the city that the Romans hadn't built. In the boring bits of the service, I'd look around at the strong pillars and round arches that were painted in the sort of bright and beautiful colours I hardly ever saw anywhere else; not even in the dye vats at home where we coloured the leather. Then, after the service was over, I was allowed some time to myself and I'd run outside knowing that the rest of the day was my own.

At these times I'd often meet up with Matty. Her real name is Matilda but no one actually calls her that. She's the same age as me and has been a servant in our house for as long as I can remember. But she's actually much more than just a servant. In a way, she's like my third sister and we've played together since we were both very little. None of us could have imagined life without her. So when it was decided my mother and sisters should go south to Wessex, it was also decided that Matty would stay with us in

Eoforwick to help run the house and keep everything as normal as possible.

Most Sundays after Mass, Matty and I would run back home and collect Ranulph, our guard dog. His name means 'house wolf' and he looks fiercer than any wild creature of the woods. But really he's as soft and friendly as a kitten and liked nothing better than to play with the piece of old leather that Mother had stitched into a ball for him. Matty and I would throw it across the big yard at the back of our house, which stands on a side street not far from one of the main gates into the city. Most of the houses are built of wood with thatched roofs, but many of the old Roman stone buildings are also still standing and still in use. Our house has stone walls and, though the roof is thatched now, most of it was built by the Romans.

Sometimes when we were playing with Ranulph, he'd bark so loudly that Mother would make us take him out into the streets. We'd run off to the open spaces behind some of the old Roman walls and throw his ball for him, or go exploring through some of the alleys and streets where no one lived. At the time we had no idea how important these games and explorations would be. But one day they would save our lives.

My aunt in Norwic continued to send

messages to us about the Viking Army whenever she got the chance and, as soon as a letter arrived, Mother and Father would go to their chamber and discuss whatever she'd sent.

Over time, the letters from my aunt became almost normal and I hardly took any notice when they arrived. But one day she sent word that the Vikings were getting ready to move out and everything changed. The King of East Anglia had kept the peace with the invaders by helping them and by paying them gold, and now we learned that he'd also even given them horses so that the Great Army could move much more quickly! I suppose this was a clever thing to do because at least it meant that the Vikings left East Anglia. But now everyone else just had to hold their breath and wait to see where they'd go next!

CHAPTER THREE

In the end my parents decided that the best thing to do was to take no chances and, rather than wait to see where the Vikings attacked next, my mother and sisters left for Wessex on a cold day in October. It was just before All Souls' Day – an important time in the church that, for me, began the long lead up to Christmas.

A line of carts stood outside the gates of the buildings that made up our leather works as well as our home. My mother was giving orders and making sure the carts were properly packed. It looked as though half of all our belongings were going south to

Wessex. This was only a bit of an exaggeration, because not only were my mother and sisters taking their own personal belongings with them, they were also taking some equipment used in the making of leather. My father's brother, Uncle Cerdic, had his own works, and our equipment would make the partnership bigger and better.

My mother was also taking with her two of our oldest servants who had a long experience of leather making, but who probably would have been useless if the Viking Army did march north.

After she'd finished making sure the old men were safely settled in one of the carts, she turned to look back at our home, hands on hips, and spotted me.

"Aldwyn!" She called sharply. "Come here and say goodbye to your mother and sisters!"

I scuttled forward and hugged her. Like a lot of Saxon women, my mother was always in control. I've never known anyone argue with her … well not more than once anyway.

A cold wind howled down the small side

street where our home stood and she pulled the collar of my tunic closed. "Where's your cloak?" she demanded. "You're going to be no help to your father if you fall ill."

"I'll go and get it," I answered.

"No don't bother, there's no time now. Say goodbye to your sisters."

Cwen was standing next to the leading cart, an almost perfect smaller copy of Mother. She was a year older than me and bossy. She was taller than me too, with hair the colour of straw and a tongue that never stopped telling people what to do. Still, like Mother, she was also kind in a gruff sort of way, and when I walked up she smiled.

"Goodbye, Aldwyn. Keep safe, look after Dad and don't take any risks."

She was always giving orders but, for the first time, I realized I was going to miss her. "You keep safe too. Be careful on the roads

– it's a long way to Wessex."

"It'll be even longer the way we're going," she answered. "Mother says we're heading towards Wales before we turn properly south. Then we're going to follow the border as we travel through Mercia. That way we should be safe from the Vikings."

I nodded and smiled. Then, for the first time since we were very little children, I hugged her. The house would seem very empty without Cwen and her bossiness.

My youngest sister, Meryl, was already sitting in the cart. At nine years old she was everything Cwen wasn't: quiet, small and as delicate as the singing bird she was named after. She looked frightened as she waited to begin the journey.

I reached up and took her hand. "Bye, Meryl. You're going on quite an adventure!"

"Yes, but I want to stay here!" she answered in a voice that was almost a whisper.

"But you'll love it in Wessex," I said, trying to encourage her. "Uncle Cerdic is funny and kind, and … and … it's warmer in the south," I added as the freezing wind suddenly whipped down the street again.

That seemed to cheer her up a bit, and she smiled as she pulled her cloak closer around her shoulders.

Dad came out of the house then, interrupting us. Ranulph, our guard dog, was following him, his head hanging low because he knew some of his people were going away. I also knew I'd have to spend all day comforting him as he whined for Cwen and Meryl.

"Well, it's time you were off and away," said Father in a voice he obviously hoped sounded happy.

Mother nodded, her face showing nothing, but when she kissed and hugged my father they hung on to each other like people clinging to something safe in a storm. She hugged me then, and I gasped as her strong arms drove the breath out of me.

"Be careful, Aldwyn," she said. "Your father will bring you all to Wessex at the first sign of trouble."

I nodded and stood back to watch as Cwen and Mother joined Meryl in the first cart. The driver cracked his whip and the small train of wagons creaked and groaned their way down the street heading for the city gates. Ranulph watched for a moment before throwing back his head and howling. I felt like joining in with him. Instead I took his collar, knelt down beside him and buried my face in the thick fur of his neck. I looked up to watch as the carts turned heavily out of the street and, as I waved, they disappeared from view.

CHAPTER FOUR

I waved at the empty street until my arm ached and hoped that Ranulph's whimpering would mask the fact that I was crying too. Eventually Father led the way back through the gateway and into our yard.

Matty was waiting, one of the few people I didn't mind seeing me upset. She didn't look very happy herself, and she surprised me by suddenly hugging me and then Ranulph.

"They've gone then?" she said, her voice muffled in the dog's coat.

I nodded. "Didn't you say goodbye?"

She looked up, "Yes, earlier, in the house I didn't want to be in the way when you and your father were waving them off."

"You wouldn't have been in the way. You're like family."

She took a deep breath. "Well, now the family's been separated and I'm going to make it my job to keep this part of it safe until we're all together again."

By this time Father had gone into the house and we stood with Ranulph in the yard. I knew there wouldn't be much work done for the rest of the day, so I took the plaited rope we used for a lead from its place behind the outhouse door and threaded it through Ranulph's collar. "Come on," I said. "Let's take him for a walk; it'll help him to get over Mother and the girls leaving."

Once out of the house we headed deep into the city. As usual the streets were busy with people coming and going about their business. The strange thing was, no one seemed to be discussing the Viking Army. It was almost as if we were the only ones who knew about them marching out of East Anglia. But I knew this couldn't be right because there were many merchants and traders in the city and at least some of them must have had contacts and family in areas where the Vikings had passed through. Perhaps everyone was just trying to carry on as normally as possible for as long as possible. My mother always says panic has never helped any situation.

Certainly there wasn't any panic to be seen as we walked along. It all seemed to be business as usual. Shops lined the streets, with their open stalls spilling goods out on to the road. Father said it was possible to buy everything you needed in Eoforwick, and a good deal of what you wanted too. There were mounds of vegetables everywhere, and the butchers' shops were attracting flies even on that cold day. At least the smell wasn't as bad as it could be in the summer!

But there were more than just food shops; there were jewellers selling brooches and rings in all sorts of metals, from gold for the richest people of the city, to polished iron and tin for those who had less money but who still wanted to look their best. There were also carpenters making furniture, cloth merchants and tailors, shoe makers and craftsmen who could make almost anything in leather. Some of these were my father's best customers. In fact, there were shops selling almost every sort of product you could think of in Eoforwick and all were working as usual as though the Viking Army was just a rumour that was somebody else's problem.

Well if everyone else could carry on as normal so could we! I'd remembered to bring Ranulph's ball along and, as soon as we reached one of the open spaces where older houses had fallen and no one had built any to replace them, Matty and I started to throw it for him to fetch. He loved this simple game and would happily play it for hours if he was allowed to.

Ranulph is a very big dog and his deep, excited barking echoed around the houses as he ran off to search for his ball. We watched as he dived through the heavy undergrowth of weeds, nettles and brambles that grew all over the open space.

Soon he came back with the ball clamped in his massive jaws, his long tail wagging. "Here, give it to me," said Matty. "Let's give him something to really chase!"

She took the ball and threw it with all her strength, hoping to send it deep into the tangled growth of weeds, but instead it fell well short and Ranulph leapt on it with glee. I laughed, happy to have something to distract me from the memory of Mother and

Cwen and Meryl leaving the city.

"Well, if you think you can do any better, let's see it," said Matty taking the ball from Ranulph and handing it to me.

It was wet with slobber, and I rubbed it on my leggings as I looked for an exact place to throw it. I desperately wanted to do better than Matty, not because she was a girl, but because I'd secretly been training with my father's spear and shield, and I hoped my fitness and strength was increasing. Like all able-bodied men in Northumbria, Father was a member of something called the 'fyrd', which is like an army of ordinary citizens who train to use weapons and fight so that they could defend their city if needed. In three years time when I'm fourteen I'll join the fyrd too, but already I've often been with my father to his training days and watched as the few full-time soldiers we have in Eoforwick, called 'housecarles', taught the other men how to fight. I'd been so many times, I could remember most of the training they did with spears, swords and shields, and it was this that I went through in the yard very early in the morning before anyone else was up. Father's shield was large and round, covered with black leather and edged with an iron rim. It was really heavy and for the first few weeks of my secret training I could hardly lift it. But gradually it got easier to hold it on my arm and then, with my other arm, hold the spear above my head and point it at an imaginary enemy. This wasn't easy; the spear was longer than a man was tall and difficult to balance. But I'd been training two or three times a week for more than half a year now, and I really hoped I was stronger and fitter than I had been when I first started.

I threw Ranulph's ball up and caught it again. Surely I could throw this small piece of stitched leather further than Matty. If not, I might as well not bother with the secret training and stay in bed for a little longer in the morning.

I chose a spot on the far side of the bit of ground where we were playing, drew back my spear arm and threw the ball with every bit of strength I had. It sailed in a high curve through the air like a hawk chasing a pigeon! Ranulph let out a loud bark of excitement and galloped across the ground in pursuit. The ball sailed on until it eventually fell out of sight deep amongst the brambles and nettles way across our playing ground.

"YES! YES! YES!" I shouted in triumph and excitement! I'd thrown the ball far further than I thought I ever could!

"Not bad," said Matty with a smile and, being the kind girl she was, she patted me hard on the back. "Come on, let's see if we can help Ranulph find it!"

All we could see of the dog was his huge tail as he searched in wide zigzags through the high tangle of weeds. He was whining with excitement like he does when chasing squirrels that always manage to get away. We dived in and joined him, taking care not to get our clothes snagged on the brambles and avoiding as far as possible the huge clumps of stinging nettles.

Ranulph disappeared ahead of us and after a few moments sent up a tumble of excited barks. "I think he's found the ball," I said, and Matty nodded.

We headed for the noise, wading through the weeds that were getting thicker and deeper. Ranulph barked again, but this time the sounds were strangely hollow, as though he was in a well or a cave.

We pushed on and suddenly the undergrowth gave way and we found ourselves walking over what looked like an old yard that was paved with wide, flat pieces of rock or flagstones. "Must be an old Roman place," I said looking at the stonework.

Matty nodded, "And look there," she said pointing ahead.

A few paces further on stood a crumbling stone wall almost hidden by a stand of truly ancient apple trees. "This might have been somebody's orchard once," I said, but before we could discuss it further, Ranulph reappeared, his leather ball in his mouth and his tail wagging furiously.

He leapt around us in excitement for a while, but eventually we calmed him down and Matty walked over to the old wall. "I think there's something hidden here," she said and started to pull at the branches of a fallen apple tree. Ranulph and I joined her, and together we forced our way through until we could see a rounded arch built into the wall. It was just like the arches in the cathedral, but instead of being at the top of stone columns that held up a roof, this arch just rose up directly from the ground and looked like the sun setting over the sea when half of it has sunk under the water.

"It's the entrance to a tunnel of some sort!" said Matty excitedly.

I peered through the archway into darkness but, as my eyes adjusted, I could see shafts of light coming down from what must have been holes in the tunnel's roof. "Come on, let's explore!"

CHAPTER FIVE

Matty was easily as brave as any boy and she nodded. But she insisted that we put Ranulph on his lead first. We didn't want him disappearing into the shadows.

The tunnel was high enough to stand up in and, as far as we could tell, it ran downhill quite steeply. We stood just inside the entrance for a few moments while our eyes adjusted to the gloom, and then we set off. Dust was dancing in the shafts of light coming down from holes in the ceiling, but they didn't seem to be caused by damage of any sort. In fact when we reached the first one, we looked up and could clearly see that the hole was neatly edged with stone as though it had been put there deliberately and for a reason.

The place smelt damp and muddy – not surprisingly – and water dripped constantly. There were also lots and lots of smaller tunnels that led off to either side, but these were much lower than the main tunnel where we were, and some of them were so low you would have had to crawl if you wanted to explore them. But every one of these side shafts had arches just like the one we'd come through, except that these arches were made of red tiles. So, obviously, all of the tunnels had been made by the Romans. But what were they for?

It had been raining and snowing over the last few days, and there were small streams of water running out of the side tunnels and into the main one, where it continued to flow down the hill we were following.

"I wonder where it leads to," said Matty. "Let's see how far we can get before we have to turn back. These holes in the roof let in enough light, so there shouldn't be any problems."

I wasn't so sure there wouldn't be problems, but agreed anyway, and we set off.

The tunnel continued downhill, and in one place the stone blocks that made up the sides and roof of the tunnel had fallen in so that we could see the sky. But the way wasn't blocked, and we climbed over the rubble and carried on down the tunnel.

Ranulph had been quiet most of the time and had his nose pressed firmly to the ground as he followed one scent after another. I still had him on the lead, which was a good job because at one point he dived for one of the smaller side tunnels and, even though I tried to hold him back, he pulled me quite a way in.

When I finally managed to stop him, I looked around and found that, though the place was much smaller than the main route, I could stand up. Matty joined us and started to help me drag Ranulph out. It was hard work because, as much as we wanted him out, he wanted to stay. He thought it was a sort of game and barked happily as we hauled on his lead, and he hauled back.

We ended up with the giggles, especially when I fell over and got covered in the thick, smelly brown mud that we'd been splashing through ever since we came into the tunnel. We stopped for a rest and looked up to where daylight came in through a hole in the roof. The hole was at the top of a shaft that was lined with blocks of stone just like the rest of the tunnel.

"It really stinks in here," Matty said. "And so do you now."

I nodded and looked down at my tunic and leggings. "Dad's not going to be very happy with me."

"Well you won't be able to sneak in and get changed before he sees you; he'll be able to smell you coming!"

"The entire city will," I agreed. "What is this stuff anyway, it can't just be mud?"

"You know, it smells like…" Matty paused. "Actually, I don't like to say what it smells like!"

She wrinkled her nose and started to giggle again. Then she stopped and looked up the shaft to the hole. "You know, that hole and this smell… It's like … it's like we're standing at the bottom of a privy."

I stared at her "You mean … you mean someone sat up there and did their business and it came down here into these tunnels? No!"

"Yes!" said Matty. "There must've been more water down here then and it washed out of here into the main tunnel and then … and then it went somewhere else."

I stared at her open-mouthed. "So this whole system of tunnels was nothing but one gigantic privy?! But why?"

She paused and frowned as she thought. "Well, it's obviously Roman. Look at all the stonework and tiles. Perhaps there were more people in the city then and they had to get rid of the muck somehow. And it's got to be better than just doing it in a hole like we do and then covering it with earth and digging a new hole when it's full. It's really clever when you think about it."

I looked down at myself. "Do you mean I'm covered in Roman muck that's hundreds of years old?"

Matty nodded and started to giggle again. After a few moments of feeling a bit sick, I started to giggle too and then Ranulph added his happy barks so that it must have sounded like a group of madmen had decided to make a home underground.

Eventually we stopped and this time we managed to drag Ranulph back to the main tunnel. Matty peered ahead along the long shaft in front of us and looked thoughtful. "I think I can guess where it goes now."

"Where?" I asked.

"Come on, I'll show you."

We went on and after a while we saw light ahead, but this time it was coming along the tunnel rather than down from holes in the roof. We walked quickly on and soon we came to another wide archway that was just like the one where we'd first started at the top of the passageway.

"I can smell the river!" I said

"Exactly," said Matty smugly. "Come on, I'll show you." She led the way to the entrance and, along with Ranulph, forced her way through a thick tangle of reeds and other plants to stand on the bank of the River Ouse.

As I joined them, I realized that the

tunnel came out beyond the city walls. It was actually built into the stone at the foot of part of the wall that ran next to the river. Also, judging by the broken rusty iron around it, the tunnel had once had heavy iron bars over it to stop anyone getting in.

We looked out across the water to the quaysides and landing stages where some merchants had their goods delivered by boat rather than using the roads. The river was one of the most important ways into and out of the city, so it was always busy.

"Don't you see?" said Matty. "This is where all of it ended up: in the river where it was washed away."

I nodded. "Great, but now we've got to get home without dad seeing or smelling the mess I'm in."

"Yeah," she agreed. "The hem of my dress isn't much cleaner, and the same can be said about my shoes."

"And Ranulph looks like he's been rolling in it!" I added.

The answer to the last problem was easy. We washed the dog in the river and used my cloak to dry him. Then we made our way home by climbing up from the bank and then through the nearest gate and on to the streets we knew like the backs of our hands.

As we entered the city, we couldn't help but notice that carts and wagons filled the roads to the brim. The street leading down to the gates was completely blocked by them and the noise of drivers shouting and arguing with each other about who had the right of way echoed back from the surrounding houses.

Earlier when we'd walked through the city I thought everyone was carrying on as normal despite the rumours of the Great Viking Army coming our way, but now I could see that many people were leaving. Perhaps, like us, they were sending some family members to safety, while others stayed on to look after businesses and property in Eoforwick.

I suppose this was a sensible thing to do, but somehow I couldn't help feeling that our homes were being slowly abandoned. If the Vikings really were planning to attack the city, shouldn't we stay and defend our homes? Shouldn't we fight? But then I remembered what Dad had told me about the enemy. They were all full-time soldiers with years of fighting experience behind them after invading countries throughout Europe. We'd have no chance against them. It was better to get as many of our people to safety as we could and then fight back when we were ready.

Dad once told me that you can lose almost every battle and still win the war, as long as you win the last battle. Perhaps that's what we were going to do.

CHAPTER SIX

We made our way through the crowded roads as best we could, and then, when we were able to slip into the clearer side streets, I turned to Matty.

"We're not the only ones who've heard about the Viking Army, then," I said as we watched what looked like an entire family of mother, father, children and two old grannies trundling slowly along in the traffic.

But we still had to get back without anyone seeing what a muddy mess we were in, so we quickly made our way home. When we got to the street where our house stood, we hurried to the tall and wide gates protected the way into the tannery. The gates stood a little open and, though I could hear some noises coming from the sheds, there was no sign of Father. Quickly, we slipped in and hurried off to the main house.

Mother was always proud of our home. Like most houses we had a main hall where we gathered and sat, told stories, chatted about our days and generally lived as a family when we weren't working. The walls and few windows were covered with cloth hangings that my mother and sisters had decorated with stitched patterns and designs. A fire burned in a stone-lined pit in the middle of the floor, and along the sides of the hall there were the raised platforms where we had our beds. These were covered with curtains that Mother and the girls had also decorated with patterns. I tried not to let

myself wonder whether I'd ever see them again as I quickly took off my filthy tunic, leggings and shoes and fetched clean things from my clothes chest that stood next to my sleeping platform. Then I hurried out into the yard where Matty was already waiting with a bundle of her clothes. We immediately took them into the shed where we kept the washtub and dumped them in the large barrel.

"There. I'll wash them later with all the other household stuff," said Matty.

I breathed a sigh of relief. Dad would never guess what we'd been doing now. Mother wouldn't have been as easy. Nothing ever got past her – she would have immediately noticed that Matty and I had changed our clothes and then demanded to know why.

But thinking of Dad reminded me that he wasn't anywhere to be seen. I knew he wasn't in the house, and when I checked in the tanning sheds, there were only the men, Anlaf and Osgar, preparing hides.

Perhaps he'd gone off on some business or other, as he sometimes did. In the end, I decided that he'd come back when he was ready, and Matty and I went off to our usual jobs around the household; me to help Anlaf and Osgar in the tanning sheds, and Matty to start preparing food for the evening meal.

Dad came back just as it was getting dark, and later that night I sat with him in the hall. We sat on our stools staring into the flames of the fire. Ranulph was quiet and lay close to the fire happily warming himself.

"I went with some of the other merchants to try and see the Ealdormen today," Dad suddenly said, taking me by surprise. So that's where he'd been all day. The Ealdormen were a group of older men who, along with the king, ruled the city and all of Northumbria. Dad didn't often tell me important things, but I suppose with Mother away he had no one else to talk to.

"Oh yes," I answered uncertainly. "Why?"

He looked up. "Some of the other merchants and I wanted to make sure they'd heard the rumours about the Viking Army coming north towards the city."

"Surely they must have," I said. "If we know, and the other people of the city also know, important people like them must do too?"

Dad shrugged. "I suppose so, but we never got to see them. The housecarles wouldn't let us in. They wouldn't listen to us either. Whenever we tried to say anything about the Vikings they just ignored us, and when we kept trying, they got ugly and told us to … well, to go away otherwise they'd make us."

I nodded; even at my age I'd noticed that housecarles thought themselves better than most other people. They were professional soldiers; that's all they did. They didn't have other jobs like weaving or tanning or farming, they just practised being soldiers all day. The Viking Army was exactly the same, but there were many more of them and, because they nearly always fought against men who were soldiers for only part of the time, they won every battle.

"Perhaps the housecarles knew that the Ealdormen had already been told about the Vikings and didn't want to disturb them," I said hopefully.

Dad shrugged again. "Perhaps. But if they don't know, then I'm afraid for this city. No one thinks that merchants and traders know anything about war, but we need a peaceful market to sell our goods in, so we always know when armies are marching and people are running away from them. The people with power would be wise to listen to us."

I'd heard Dad say this many times so I just nodded. After that we sat in the enormous silence of our home without Mother and the girls, and eventually I went to bed. I secretly let Ranulph join me when Dad wasn't looking and, after he'd curled up in a tight ball at the bottom of the bed, I settled down and soon fell asleep, exhausted after our day of explorations.

CHAPTER SEVEN

The next day dawned bright and sunny but very cold. I got dressed quickly and was just wondering what to do about breakfast when Matty came in with a pile of logs that she laid in the hearth on the embers of yesterday's fire.

"Pull up a stool and sit down. I've made us porridge."

"Where's Dad?" I called after her as she disappeared out of the door.

"Somewhere," she called back unhelpfully.

When she came back carrying a pot with two smaller bowls placed over the top like a double lid, I tried again. "Does anyone know where Dad is?"

"Anlaf and Osgar say he went out early to see if there's any news."

"And is there?"

Matty looked at me as though I was daft. "I don't know, he's not back yet."

I grinned at her frowning face. "I'll have lots of porridge; it'll keep out the cold."

"You'll have what you're given," she answered, but then spooned a huge serving out of the pot and into our bowls. Matty made good porridge, it was thick and hot – instead of boiling it up with water and then flavouring it with salt as is usual, she had a special way of making it with milk and adding honey and even a few spices we bought from the merchants who had shops near the river.

Ranulph had his own bowl and he slurped up his serving in two or three big gulps and then sat and stared at us as we ate. But we made a point of ignoring him.

"So I suppose it'll be just a normal day … as long as the Viking Army doesn't attack," I added.

"Not funny," said Matty.

"No," I agreed.

But I was wrong about it being a normal day. Dad got back not long after we'd finished breakfast and, after telling us there was no news, he then told me to get the handcart ready and take a delivery of vellum – the very fine calf's leather used for making the pages of books – to the cathedral, and I was to take Matty along to help. Usually Dad handled all dealings with the cathedral's scriptorium – the place where the books were made – but he was obviously distracted by the threat of the Viking Army.

Ranulph was very upset when we left

him behind, but animals aren't allowed in churches, apart from cats who keep the mice under control.

I fetched the handcart from the storage shed and we began to load it with the fine vellum in the main yard. There wasn't actually that much to carry because vellum is very expensive and, though the scriptorium is always busy, it takes a very long time to actually make a book. Not only do the words have to be written, but there are usually lots of pictures and decorations to add as well.

As soon as we'd loaded the cart, we headed out into the street and towards the cathedral. It's only a short distance away, and you can see the towers of the huge church quite easily if you stand in our main yard.

The streets were quiet, unlike the day before when many carts had been heading out of the city. I mentioned this to Matty and she shrugged. "Anyone who was going to leave has obviously gone by now." She said. I nodded. "We'll just have to see if they were right to go or not."

"Yes," Matty agreed. "But I have to say that I certainly hope they're wrong."

"Me too; if they're right we'll be having the Vikings as visitors whether we like it or not!"

We arrived at the rear of the cathedral where the goods are usually delivered. The cathedral was actually a very good customer to lots of merchants throughout the city. Not only did all the priests and everyone else have to be fed, but they needed all sorts of other supplies too. It was like a small city in its own right.

The man who met us in the delivery yard had an expression on his face that made it look like someone had pushed a piece of stinking fish up his nose! He made it pretty obvious that he didn't trust us, or any other merchant for that matter, and made a point of examining every bit of vellum before he reluctantly nodded his head and called a young serving boy to carry it into the scriptorium.

That done, we had some time to ourselves and we decided to use it by exploring the cathedral. Both Matty and I knew the place well and went there for every big festival and service, but there was always something new to see, such as a bit of new carving the stonemasons had made, or sometimes a new priest making a fool of himself as he nervously worked his way through a service; there might also be a cathedral cat basking in a pool of sunlight on the flagstoned floor or the gleam and glitter of beautiful silver chalices (or cups) on the altar, and there were always people everywhere as they came to say their prayers, meet friends and have a good gossip.

We walked through the huge doors that stood open despite the cold weather, and into the massive space between the roof, high above our heads, and the stone floor beneath our feet. This was one of the few stone buildings in the city that hadn't been made by the Romans, but we could see echoes of their work in the thick columns that soared to the roof and the round-topped arches that held it up, just like the ones we'd seen in the tunnel only the day before. Obviously the people who had built the cathedral had looked at the work of the Romans and had recreated it, but in a slightly different way; in a way that was our own.

The place was busy and noisy with people who were all rushing about to get the cathedral ready for the important All Hallows Day ceremony that would happen the following day on November 1st. This is one of the main celebrations in the lead-up to Christmas and usually the Ealdormen and rulers of Northumbria would be there. It'd be interesting to see how many would actually attend with the threat of the Viking Army hanging over us.

Matty and I stood in the middle of the main floor – my mother told me it was called a nave – and watched the people swirl around us as they swept and scrubbed the floors, freshened the paint on the brightly coloured pillars and other stonework where it was needed, and even washed the statues. We giggled when we saw a tall bearded figure of a saint having his stone face washed, just like a naughty child who'd got honey round his mouth after raiding the food store.

But eventually the swirling masses of people began to become just a confusing tangle and we started to get bored, so we decided to go home before Dad missed us. There was still plenty of work to do, even if the Viking Army was on the march.

It was probably because we were thinking of soldiers and war that we noticed there were housecarles everywhere throughout the cathedral as we left. For a moment, it gave me comfort to see these professional fighters who guarded the Ealdormen and important buildings of the city in such threatening times. But then Matty shook her head: "They're saying in the markets that there are ten times more soldiers in the Viking Army than we have housecarles, and not only that, but the Vikings are hardened fighters who've fought wars in France and other countries before they came here."

"Well, what does that matter?" I snapped, annoyed that she'd spoilt my little daydream about the housecarles keeping us safe.

"It matters a lot when most of our soldiers have spent their time doing nothing but guarding buildings and fat old men. And even those who have been in wars have only fought against the half-trained fyrd – part-time soldiers who go home to bake the bread or stitch shoes when they've finished their bit of practice."

"What do you know about it?" I said, getting really annoyed. "You're just a girl and I'm just a boy, we're too young to understand! And ... and anyway, I'm sure the important people have thought of all of that!"

"Well a lot of the folk I hear talking in the markets aren't just boys and girls!" Matty snapped back. "And what about your dad? He's been saying exactly the same for days now!"

She was right of course. I'd heard terrible stories about what the Viking Army did when they attacked and captured a city. Some said they killed every man of fighting age, which meant all men between the ages of fourteen and sixty! And I don't suppose they'd ask a boy like me when my birthday was before they stabbed me! It was too terrible to think about, so I just closed my mouth, shook my head and hurried home.

CHAPTER EIGHT

Ranulph met us at the gate and jumped around barking as we wheeled the handcart we'd carried the vellum on back into the yard. Dad was working in the sheds, but he came out when he heard us arrive.

He nodded when we told him we'd delivered the vellum safely, but looked grim when we described the preparations for All Souls' Day in the cathedral.

"Let's just hope they've spent as much time getting the defence of the city ready," he muttered to himself, and then without another word he took off the thick leather apron he wore when working in the sheds and went out.

We watched him go and then looked at each other. "He's not happy," I said. "I wonder where he's going."

"Perhaps he's going to try and talk with the Ealdormen again," Matty suggested.

"I don't think there's much chance of that," I answered, ready to talk about the Viking threat again now that I'd seen how Dad felt. "They're too busy with the cathedral."

After that we went off to our different tasks. It seemed strange carrying on with the usual routine when our home could be attacked at any time. But I soon realized that there was nothing else we could do. After all, the Vikings might not come anywhere near the city, and we still had a living to make.

Later that day, I met Matty in the yard

and got ready to take Ranulph for his evening run. Dad still hadn't come home, but as this was quickly becoming a normal thing, we just carried on as best we could.

We opened the gate and set off just as the sun was setting on a bright, cold day. Frost was already creeping along the ground as the shadows grew longer, and early stars were beginning to peep out in the east where the sky was darkest. Wood smoke mingled with the scent of cooking as everywhere people prepared their evening meals.

"I wonder what we'll know by the time we're cooking supper tomorrow," said Matty.

"Hopefully the same as we know now," I answered brightly, but my words echoed on the strangely empty streets, and it felt as though we were walking through a city that had been half abandoned by its people.

Ranulph barked as though he'd heard

something and growled, but even though we stopped and listened for a while, we couldn't hear anything unusual.

"Come on, you stupid hound," I said ruffling his ears. "You're barking at ghosts and shadows."

Matty looked at me with wide eyes at the mention of ghosts. But I refused to get involved in anything she might have to say about that, and I led Ranulph along the street.

"Wait for me," she suddenly shouted and ran after us. "It's getting dark already."

I stopped and waited for her and then we took Ranulph to an open piece of land just behind the city walls and spent a little time throwing his ball and letting him burn off some energy.

In the time spent between throwing the ball and waiting for Ranulph to bring it back, I looked closely at the condition of the defences, just to see if the Ealdormen had done anything about repairing and strengthening them. But there was no sign of any work being done. It was almost as though the king and his advisors knew nothing of the Viking threat. No wonder Dad was so grumpy. Unless something was done to repair the walls now, the enemy could easily break into the city and we could all be killed in our beds!

CHAPTER NINE

When I went to bed I expected to lie awake all night, but I surprised myself by waking up the next morning after a long dreamless sleep. It was strangely dark because heavy clouds had settled over the city, and when I got dressed and went out into the yard, I noticed that the clouds were so low that I couldn't see the tops of the twin cathedral towers that stood either side of the main doorway and rose high into the sky. It felt and looked like late afternoon. And the fact that it was All Souls' Day made it worse because it was a holiday and so there wasn't the usual early morning bustle and noise as people got ready for work.

I'd heard Dad come back late the night before, but he'd obviously got up very early and gone out again. Perhaps he'd decided to go to the early Mass in the cathedral rather than wait for the main ceremony that would be attended by all the Ealdormen and other important people. I couldn't really blame him – it would be crowded and noisy and full of the sort of people who used religious holidays as an excuse to show off their wealth by wearing their most expensive clothes and finest jewellery.

Ranulph bounded up to me then with a happy bark, but even his huge voice fell flat on the strangely dark morning. It was almost as if the low clouds were smothering the city. And then, just as Matty appeared with our breakfast, a tiny wisp of snow wandered down from the sky.

"First snow of the winter," said Matty. "That's lucky."

"For who?" I asked.

"For us, I hope," she answered, a look on her face that said she was determined to be happy no matter what.

"The snows are earlier than usual. Is that a good omen?" I asked.

After breakfast we both decided to go up on to the city walls. As I've already said, All Souls' Day is a holiday, so apart from washing the few pots, we were free to do as we wanted, until that is we had to go to the service in the cathedral.

As soon as we opened the gates, Ranulph shot out ahead of us barking madly. I was surprised by this because, apart from when he was playing, he was usually a fairly quiet dog, but he seemed to be affected by the strange atmosphere that hung heavily over the city like the clouds.

The streets were almost completely deserted and, even though the sun would be climbing the sky by this time, the light was still struggling against the shadows.

"It's almost like there are two cities," Matty suddenly said as we walked along.

"What do you mean?" I asked

"Well look at the place; most of the merchants and traders seem to have sent their families away, and yet the really rich are still here, getting ready for the service in the cathedral and carrying on as if everything is normal."

"It's not only the rich that are still here," I said, nodding at a beggar who sat on the corner of the street.

"No, but the poor have no choice, they've got to stay; they can't afford to get away."

I'd let Ranulph off his lead and he trotted

ahead of us following scents and stopping to sniff anything that interested him. "You know, sometimes I think it must be easier to be a dog than it is to be a boy or a girl. Look at him, he's as happy as anything just so long as he has enough food, his people with him and his leather ball to play with."

Matty nodded. "Perhaps there's a lesson to be learned from animals. If we were all happy with what we had, then perhaps we wouldn't want to take things from others and send armies to do it. As long as we had enough, of course."

By this point we'd reached the long winding street that ran behind the ramparts or walls of the city. Most of them were made of stone and had been built by the Romans, but at points where the stones had crumbled away over the long years, high wooden fences had been built to fill the gaps. None of these were in very good condition and should have been replaced, especially now with the Viking threat, but Northumbria was one of the most powerful kingdoms in the whole island of Britain, and so there'd been no real threat to the main city of Eoforwick, no real reason to keep the defences in good repair … until now.

We came to one of the sets of steps that led up to the walkway on the walls and we quickly climbed up. We'd chosen a section that was still strongly built of stone, and we stood under the top edge and then scrambled up to sit in the space between two higher sections of wall that soldiers could shelter behind when the walls were attacked. We even managed to drag Ranulph up beside us by hauling on his collar and giving him a hoist behind his back legs.

All three of us looked out over the flat

land that surrounded the city. From here we could see that the low clouds hung dark and threatening over the entire area as far as the eye could see. Which actually wasn't very far because it was so gloomy, and the snow was still slowly falling making the view hazy and unclear. Here and there small stands of woodland loomed up as darker shadows against the grey, and we could also see the thin black lines of hedgerows that divided up the surrounding area into fields.

"What's that over there," Matty suddenly said pointing out over the land.

"Where?" I asked following her pointing finger.

"Just there, where the clouds seem to touch the land."

"I can't see anything," I said, screwing up my eyes and staring as hard as I could.

Matty continued to gaze in silence for a moment and then shook her head. "It's gone now. I thought I saw something moving over the land … something big."

"Big?" I questioned. "Like an army, perhaps?"

She shook her head. "No, I can't see anything now. I must have imagined it."

I looked along the walls for a housecarle or ordinary member of the fyrd, so that we could report that we might have seen something, but there was no one else in sight.

Even I, an eleven-year-old boy, thought that it might have been a good idea to put some of the housecarles on the highest points as lookouts. But obviously I must have been wrong, because the Ealdormen didn't seem to think it was necessary.

CHAPTER TEN

Not long after that we went back down into the streets and, after a quick game of throw with Ranulph, we went back home. Dad was there, standing in the middle of the yard and looking over the rooftops to the cathedral. He must have been there for some time because the slowly falling snow had had time to settle on him, covering his cloak in white flecks.

"Ah, there you are," he said when he saw us. "Look, I think something's going to happen today and I want us to be ready for it if it does."

"Something's going to happen," I repeated

as I gave Ranulph his bowl of water. "Like what?"

"You know as much as me," Dad answered. "We might have to protect the house and the other buildings, so I want you and Matty to get up on the roof and keep a lookout. If you see anything unusual, shout as loud as you can."

I nodded and noticed for the first time that Dad had taken his spear and shield down from the wall where they usually hung and had leaned them against the shed nearest to the big gate that led out into the street. He went off into the house then and I heard him opening chests as though he was packing.

I looked at Matty and, without a word, we fetched extra cloaks to keep us warm in the bitter weather and falling snow, and then climbed up on to the roof. It wasn't difficult, the thatch made of reeds reached almost down to the ground and it was just a matter of hoisting Matty up until she had a good foothold and then grabbing her hand and following after.

We made our way to the very top and sat with our legs straddling either side of the sloping roof. From here the world looked completely different; we could see the end of the street and part of the road that led down to the nearest city gate. If anyone came along either the road or the street we'd see them and could shout a warning. Of course by 'anyone' I meant Vikings, but just saying the word, even in my own head, seemed dangerous.

Then, strangely, our world settled into a sense of peace for the first time in days. It must have been something to do with looking at everything from the rooftop and so from a different angle. But whatever the reason, my head seemed to clear of all the worry, fear and upset and I started to wonder exactly why the Viking Army was attacking us. What gave them the right to invade countries and kill people? What made them think that they could destroy buildings and lives just because they wanted to? And who said they could take other people's property and belongings?

I put these questions to Matty who was huddled up in her cloak and looked like a giant raven against the gloomy sky and the slowly falling snow. Of course, I didn't think she'd be able to give me any answers, but even so I waited to hear what she'd have to say.

"I don't know why the Vikings attack places," she said at last, just as I expected. But then she went on: "Because they can, I suppose. Perhaps because they believe if we can't defend what is ours we don't have the right to keep it."

"That can't be right," I said. "If I see a rich old man who's too weak to protect his money and wealth, I don't have the right to take it from him! The law wouldn't allow it! It'd be just plain wrong!"

Matty shrugged then nodded. "Yes, but perhaps it's different between countries."

"Well, it shouldn't be. There should be laws against it."

"And who would make the countries obey those laws?" She asked.

"I don't know… other countries?"

"I don't think that would work. Countries are like some people; they're selfish and only think of themselves."

We both fell into a gloomy silence and then Matty went on: "Anyway, I've heard some say that long ago our people were like the Vikings and that we came here after the Romans left and took the land from the folk who were here before us."

"Really?" I asked, my heart sinking. I didn't like to think of my people as pirates and murderers. I sighed and looked across the rooftops to the cathedral. In the gloom the windows glowed with lamps and candlelight, and the slowly falling snow had settled on the carvings and statues that covered the high walls so that they stood out almost as though a clever artist had painted all the edges in white. Could people who were once as violent as the Vikings really make something so beautiful?

And then I remembered that once a merchant ship came to the city from Denmark, the same country the Vikings come from. It had sailed up the river and started to trade gold, silver and bronze jewellery. And though most of us only knew rumours of the Vikings as fierce warriors and destroyers of lives, these rings and brooches and bracelets were truly beautiful with complicated patterns and strange beasts all brilliantly worked in metal and precious jewels. So there I suppose I had at least one answer to my questions: could people who destroyed and robbed and killed also make things of beauty? Yes, they obviously could.

I looked at the cathedral again as these thoughts ran through my head, and then suddenly realized that most people who were left in the city would be at the All Souls' Day service now, either in the cathedral itself or in one of the other churches. The streets were almost empty, and we'd already seen there was nobody on the walls, or at least nobody on the section we'd been on.

But before I could think any more about this, Matty nudged me. "Can you hear something?" she whispered.

I sat still for a moment and listened to the city that was as quiet as I'd ever heard it. All I could hear was Ranulph down in the yard, quietly whining because he wanted to join us on the roof. And apart from that there was nothing to be heard but the gently moaning wind and the distant call of crows and ravens.

"What am I listening for?" I asked at last.

"It sounds like…" Matty began and paused as she tried to think of the right words. "It sounds like somebody trying to be quiet … but not just one somebody … it sounds like lots of somebodies!"

I stared, ready to laugh at her. But then I heard it. A low murmuring sound, like quiet voices mixed with the noise that lots of bits of metal would make if they were being carried carefully so that they didn't clink together too much. Bits of metal like swords and axes and spearheads. It hung in the air, brought on the wind just for a moment and then it was gone.

"That, you mean?" I asked, my voice a strangled whisper.

She nodded. The sound came again mingled on the wind with the scent of wood-smoke from the many fires keeping homes warm throughout the city.

"Let's go to the end of the street and see what's happening at the gate," Matty suddenly said.

There was a clear view of the gate from the corner, so I looked quickly down into the yard and, after making sure there was nobody about, I nodded and we slid down the thatch and dropped the short distance on to the roadway.

We ran to the corner and peered round. The road was empty and the gateway loomed up into the dark sky like a giant mouth. We could clearly see that the gates themselves were closed and that the heavy wooden bar had been drawn across.

"Perhaps we'd better go back..." I began, but then my words were drowned as suddenly the world seemed to be split apart by a huge yell that roared into the air.

The Viking war-cry!

The Viking war-cry roaring from thousands of throats!

This was quickly followed by an ear-splitting crack and crash as the city gates were hit by something massively heavy.

"It's a battering ram!" I yelled over the noise. "Tell Dad!"

But instead of running back home, we both stayed rooted to the spot as though unable to move. The streets were still oddly empty. Then at last we heard running feet and the first of the city's housecarles appeared, rushing madly towards the terrible noise.

The massive hammering of the battering ram went on, booming like a huge drum into the air. But the gates, like the rest of the defences, were old and in bad condition, and suddenly there was a groaning, creaking, tearing crack as they were broken open.

"THEY'RE IN! THE VIKINGS ARE IN THE CITY!!!" I shouted. But my voice was lost in the great roar of triumph from thousands of Viking throats.

I watched in horror as suddenly the enemy appeared! They all wore the same cone-shaped iron helmet with a nose guard, and some had whole tunics made of what looked like fine chains. They moved as smoothly as oiled cogs in the lifting machines used to empty the cargo ships down on the river. Their round shields were all painted red and overlapped as closely as scales on a giant fish or dragon and they pushed forward in step almost as though they were one massive creature. A single figure in the centre of the wall of shields raised his spear and pointed, and as one, the mass of Vikings smoothly turned to follow his directions. It was strangely beautiful to see, but I knew it was also deadly and dangerous, like a snake is also beautiful in the way it moves but can kill you with one strike.

Now the clash of sword, spear and axe on shield rose into the air as our housecarles tried to stop them. Screams and shouts echoed along the streets as more and more of our housecarles ran to join the fight.

But they were too late and there were too few of them.

Matty and I clung to each other as we stared along the road to where the fighting was. Our housecarles threw themselves bravely against the oncoming soldiers, their spears and swords flashing, but the Vikings couldn't be stopped. They moved forwards like the tide of the sea and, as one, they sang a fierce song with a strong rhythm that kept them fighting together, spears thrusting, swords swinging, axes hacking in smooth unison almost like a deadly dance.

Our housecarles fell back, regrouped and then with a wild yell they charged again! But they broke against the solid shield wall like pebbles thrown against a cliff. Then with a heave the enemy rolled over them and our housecarles were gone, crushed by the unstoppable power of the Viking Army.

I think I screamed, but I heard only the rhythm and chant of the enemy war-machine as they marched forwards. Now the people appeared from their houses and started to throw anything they had at the army. Pots, pans, stones from the streets in a hopeless attempt to stop them.

I let go of Matty; my head was empty of everything but the thought that they had to be stopped. I let out a yell and ran towards the line of shields. I grabbed stones and threw them, all the time shouting and screaming.

But now the army stopped and at last the shields broke apart and the machine became individual men. Our housecarles were all dead, there was no one who could stop them now and they began to spread through the city like a fire over a thatched roof.

Dozens of Viking soldiers ran down our street, smashing open doors and dragging the people out. I dropped the stones I still had in my hands and stared in horror. Two of them were working together, kicking in doors and throwing torches on to the thatch of the houses. One of them turned and saw me, he called to his friends and laughed.

I couldn't move; I could hardly breathe.

I knew I was going to die. With a shout they ran at me and I closed my eyes. Suddenly there was a huge barking and a massive animal leapt over me. It was Ranulph! He landed on one of the Vikings and his teeth closed round his throat. Then Dad and our two men Anlaf and Osgar were with him, their spears thrusting and stabbing and Dad's shield smashing like a battering ram.

Matty ran up and pulled me away towards the house. Dad, Anlaf and Ranulph joined us, the Vikings were gone and Ranulph had blood round his mouth.

"Where's Osgar?!" I shouted, but Dad shook his head.

We reached our house, slammed the gate shut and braced it with logs and anything we could find. But now we could hear more Vikings pouring into the street. The smell of burning thatch was everywhere, catching in our throats and stinging our eyes. Smoke hung in grey clouds over the yard and the sounds of desperate screams and shouting was spreading through the city.

I don't think any of us thought about how long we could defend our home. We just did what we could as each moment passed. Then suddenly a massive hammering hit the gates and we ran and leaned against them trying to hold them shut against the Vikings outside.

Then Matty screamed and pointed to where a burning torch had landed on the thatch of the roof. It immediately caught fire and then more torches began to rain down on the rest of the roof. With a great roar the fire spread everywhere. Ranulph barked madly as we ran to fetch buckets of water, but it was hopeless. The gates burst open and Vikings poured into the yard.

Dad, Ranulph and Anlaf ran to meet them and the clash of swords and spears mingled with the roar of the flames. Anlaf fell and didn't get up, and when three Vikings drove Dad back across the yard, Ranulph leapt at them, bringing one of them down.

Dad fell and Ranulph was there again, standing over him and snarling. The Vikings stopped for a moment, and then with a great roar the roof on the tanning shed fell in. The enemy turned, distracted by the noise, and then without thinking Matty and I rushed in and dragged Dad and Ranulph away before the Vikings knew what was happening.

We ran through the house, hardly able to see in the thick smoke, but then a window loomed up before us. Its shutters had been smashed in and daylight poured into the murk and smoke, lighting up an escape route. Matty led the way and we scrambled through and out into the street that ran behind the house.

For a moment we stood and stared around us, listening to the screams and shouts echoing over the city. Then amidst all the panic and fighting and death I had an idea. "This way. I know a way out!"

I grabbed Ranulph's collar and we ran. Everywhere was in uproar. Houses were burning, Vikings were kicking open doors and dragging people and their belongings out into the streets. The last of our housecarles were dead and no one was fighting to save the city. All any of us could do now was save ourselves … if we could.

I led the way through the maze of streets, Dad still had his spear and when we came to a crossroads he went ahead to make sure the way was clear. He didn't ask where we were going — like all of us he just reacted to whatever was happening at that moment.

But by this time Matty had guessed what I had in mind and, when in all the chaos of fire and fighting I paused and couldn't find the way, she took over.

"This way!" she said and led the way down a narrow alley. We ran on for what seemed like for ever, Matty and I taking it in turns to lead as first one of us and then the other remembered the way.

We hid as best we could from the gangs of Vikings as they smashed their way through houses and shops. But again and again we had to run for our lives as groups of the enemy chased us before we lost them in the maze and tangle of the streets we'd known all our lives.

Once a Viking leapt out at us and Dad and Ranulph smashed him back against the wall of a burning house. His helmet fell off and I saw the face of the enemy clearly for the first time. Before this they'd just been monsters – something unknown to be afraid of – but now I could see they were people just like us. The Viking was young, only a little older than me, and he didn't even have his man's beard yet. Ranulph snarled and

Dad raised his spear ready to strike.
The boy Viking closed his eyes and I
grabbed Dad's arm.

"No!" I screamed.

Dad paused and looked from the boy to me and lowered his spear. We took the boy's weapons and Matty took his shoes so he wouldn't be able to walk easily over the rough city streets and then we just left him.

CHAPTER ELEVEN

Not long after that we came to the wide sweep of wasteland Matty and I had been heading for. There were none of the enemy about, but by this point most of the city was burning and the screams of the dying echoed through the streets. Taking a chance, we ran across the open space and into the tangle of undergrowth on the far side. So far we'd been lucky, but if we wanted to get out of the city we had to get beyond the walls which would have meant trying to reach one of the gates through the streets that were full of the Viking Army. Or at least it would have done, if Matty and I hadn't found the old Roman tunnel a few days ago.

We pulled aside the branches of the fallen tree that hid the entrance and quickly explained to Dad where it led.

"We think it's the old Roman drains," I said. "Matty and I found them a couple of days ago; the tunnel leads down to a part of the river that's outside the walls!"

Matty nodded. "There'll be boats, we could take one and get away from the city. The Vikings won't bother us; all they want is gold and anything else they can find."

Strangely, Dad smiled. "Well done, both of you. Lead the way."

He didn't say anything more, just stepped into the tunnel and then helped Matty and me pull the branches back in place so the entrance was hidden. I watched Dad as he did this and saw that his face now showed hardly any expression at all, and I wondered if I looked the same. After all, we'd lost everything: our home, our tannery, even our city. Not only that, but Anlaf and Osgar were dead, men that I'd known all of my life! Shouldn't we have been shouting and screaming? Shouldn't we have been fighting to the death in the streets? Shouldn't we at least have collapsed before the deep and terrible sadness at the loss of so much?

Then I felt Matty's hand on my arm. "Come on," she said. "Let's go and find your mother and sisters in Wessex."

And there it was ... the reason Dad carried on; the reason I needed to carry on. We still had our family; we still had our lives to live. Ranulph barked excitedly and headed down into the shadows of the tunnel and we all followed.

Light seeped down into the passageway through the regular holes in the roof that we had seen when we'd first explored the place a few days ago, and with it came smoke from the burning houses and the sounds of screaming.

When we came to the part where the roof of the tunnel had completely collapsed we could see Vikings running about, their hands red with blood, their eyes wild with the excitement of killing. It was hard to believe that these madmen were the same ones who were part of the disciplined army that had broken into the city just that morning. Then they had moved like parts of a machine, like cogs that knew the part they had to play. Now they ran about in a frenzy, killing and burning and destroying.

I kept a tight hold on Ranulph's collar and closed my fingers round his muzzle so he couldn't bark. When the Vikings had gone, we slipped from the shadows and hurried on further down the tunnel.

When we had first found the sewer, we'd spent over an hour exploring the side passages and discussing what the place could have been. But now we had a purpose and a place to go, so we reached the huge archway at the end that led to the river far more quickly than we believed possible.

We sat and listened for a moment before we dared step out on to the river bank. But now the terrible noise of the dying city sounded much further off than it had before. I could even hear a bird singing in the distance as though my world wasn't coming to an end.

At last Dad stepped out into the light, told us to stay hidden and disappeared. I don't know how long we waited in the shadows of the old Roman sewer, but it seemed like for ever. Every now and then the wind would shift and the stink of burning houses, shops and worse would billow around us and with it came the screams of the people still trapped in the city.

But at last Dad came back and led us out on to the river bank where a boat was waiting. "It's only an old punt," he explained, pointing at the wide and flat-bottomed craft in which some merchants carry their goods over short distances. "But it'll get us away and we can find something better later on."

We didn't care what it was, we just wanted to get away from the death and destruction, so one by one we stepped down into the punt. After we'd wrestled Ranulph into the dangerously rocking boat, Dad used a long pole to push us out into the river. There were no other boats coming from the city, it was almost as though the Vikings had made a point of taking the quays and wharfs where the merchant ships used to drop off their goods and cargoes. The only other river crafts we could see were tied up and most of them had been set on fire just like the rest of the city.

The old Roman walls loomed up above us like a cliff, but no one was on them. In fact, we couldn't see anybody. But we could hear them screaming and shouting as the Vikings still rampaged through the streets. And then, as Dad drew in the pole and started to use a paddle, we could see more and more of the city – the buildings seemed to rise up into view the further away we got.

We could see bright red, orange and blue flames roaring into the air and smoke blowing and flowing on the wind to join the grey clouds that hung over it all. But then, as we watched, the smoke was blown aside like huge billowing curtains and the mighty walls of the cathedral appeared. Its towers reached high into the sky and it seemed to float like a stone ship above all the death and destruction.

We sat and watched it for a while and then Dad found another paddle and gave it to me.

"Come on," he said. "We have to get to Wessex."

I took the paddle and drove it into the water. We'd escaped a city that was lost and a new life waited for us in one of the strongest kingdoms in all the islands. Perhaps there the Saxon people could begin to fight back against their enemies; perhaps there we'd find a leader who could stand against the Viking Army.

HISTORICAL NOTE

Aldwyn, his dad, Matty and Ranulph were like many other Saxon refugees who must have fled the Vikings. Some may have escaped to the Saxon kingdom of Wessex. But their troubles didn't end there; in 870 the Great Viking Army attacked this last independent Saxon kingdom and drove its rulers into exile in the marshes. But King Alfred of Wessex was a determined man and continued to fight from a stronghold called Athelney. From there he led a fight back, attacking the Vikings in hit-and-run raids that constantly reminded the enemy that the Saxons were still prepared to fight.

Then, after several months of preparation, during which time King Alfred and his soldiers made weapons and trained hard, the Saxons launched a full-scale attack, marching out of the marshes and challenging the enemy to battle.

The fight began at a place called Eddington. The Vikings raised their shield wall, determined to kill the last Saxon king. But Alfred led his army with skill and daring, and after a long struggle the Saxons broke the Viking line, driving them back until at last the enemy ran away. They fled back to Chippenham, the very town that they had taken from Alfred months before, and after being trapped inside the walls for days, they eventually surrendered to Alfred and agreed to his peace terms.

At about the same time that Alfred regained his kingdom, the Saxon land of

Mercia also drove out the Vikings and they agreed to fight side by side with the King of Wessex. Now there was a powerful alliance that could stand against the Viking threat.

This friendship between the two lands was sealed when King Alfred's eldest daughter, Aethleflaed, married the Lord of the Mercians. An uneasy peace followed, but wars broke out again and again between the Saxons and the Vikings, and many battles were fought. London had been taken by the Vikings but the Saxons of Wessex and Mercia attacked the city and drove the enemy out.

When Alfred died in 899, he left a safe and powerful kingdom that had an unbreakable alliance with the land of Mercia. Aethelflaed herself became a great warrior, leading soldiers into battle and fighting shoulder to shoulder with her husband. In one campaign she marched against the city of Leicester and so fearsome was her reputation as a war leader that the Vikings in the city lay down their arms without a fight.

Now began a long war in which the Saxons slowly took back much of the land that the Vikings had conquered. Aethelflaed continued the plan her father had started and built many 'burghs' or fortified towns that had strong walls and well-trained soldiers to defend them. Then, when her husband became ill, Aethelflaed ruled Mercia alone. Alongside her brother Edward – who had become King of Wessex after Alfred's death – she continued the fight against the Vikings.

Eventually the enemy was defeated and, though wars continued throughout the period, the Saxons remained strong and in control of their lands.

Eoforwic was never taken back by the Saxons, and its name was changed to Jorvik before eventually becoming known as York – the name that we use today. But the Viking rulers of the city finally surrendered to Aethelflaed, acknowledging her power and accepting her as their overlord in 918. They sent messengers to 'The Lady of the Mercians' but unfortunately she had been wounded in battle leading her soldiers only days before, and she died before receiving the surrender of her enemies.